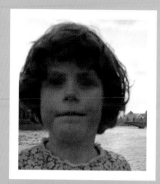

For Charles Nick Andrew and most especially, Bridget

thanks to my grandad... Robert

Thank you, Harriet, Emma, Katie, Ruth, and all of the Garrett family

with love and thanks to the real-life gorgeous morten

Copyright © 2001 by Lauren Child   All rights reserved.   First U.S. edition 2002
Library of Congress Cataloging-in-Publication Data is available.   Library of Congress Catalog Card Number 2001035069
First published in Great Britain in 2001 by Orchard Books, London   Designed by Anna-Louise Billson   ISBN 0-7636-1696-6
1 2 3 4 5 6 7 8 9 10   Printed in Singapore   Candlewick Press, 2067 Massachusetts Avenue, Cambridge, Massachusetts 02140
visit us at www.candlewick.com

Many thanks to Milo Photography for the picture of Morten

In school we are learning about the planet Earth.
Our planet Earth is large
compared to Pluto, but compared to the sun,
Earth is a peppercorn.

It's hard to think of ourselves living on a planet because it doesn't feel like we are standing on something round.

It's amazing the sea doesn't spill off at the edges, but that's gravity for you.

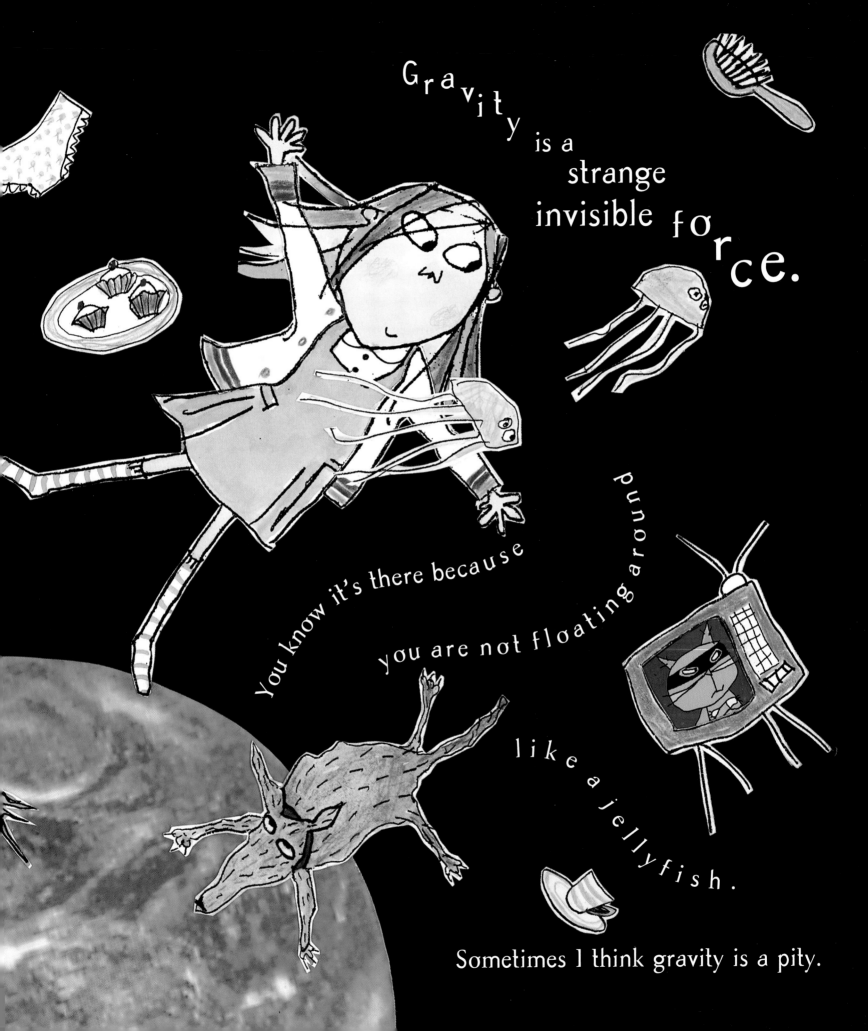

Gravity is a strange invisible force.

You know it's there because you are not floating around like a jellyfish.

Sometimes I think gravity is a pity.

Mrs. Wilberton wants us to do a project called
The Environment,
which is nature, really.

She has given us little books to write in.

Nature is something I know lots about. We've got lots of it in our backyard. There's even nature in the Baldini brothers' yard.

Although you wouldn't think so to look at it.

It's mainly trash cans and concrete and pieces of old car.

Robert Granger lives next door
    and he is always trying to walk home with me.
He says,
    Hey, Clarice Bean, **wait for me.**

Luckily,
I
am
a
fast
walker.

When I get home,
    Grandad is buttering
his tie into his sandwich.
He hasn't noticed. He's
    too busy watching a
special on nature.

Grandad loves nature,
    especially when it's Australian.
He likes the idea of living somewhe
where not many people are.
    In Australia you can drive
for maybe squillions of days
without noticing a single
        supermarket, just maybe a
kangaroo or a wombat.

He says,
I can picture myself sitting in a deck chair
on the top of Uluru,

listening to baseball on the radio.

But I'm just as happy
watching the world go by
under the tree
on Navarino Street.

That's our street.

I am busy thinking about
trees and planets and
holes
in the sky.

I am sure there is a big hole above our house
because my sister Marcie
uses too much hair spray
and is causing pollution.

spray 'n' hold

No ideas
are coming into my head
for a project.

My mind is a **blanket**.

So I go off
and read my comics
with the T-shirts and undies
in the laundry room.
(Dad says,
If it's **nature**
you are after, you should
take a peek at Kurt's bedroom.
It's a regular safari in there.)

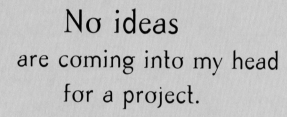

I am reading away when
I hear a commotion.
It's coming from
the kitchen.

So
I scriggle
out
to see
what's
going
on.

What's happened is, my brother Kurt has rushed in and I can see right away that he's not

normal because he is **running.** (He never runs.) He is flapping the local newspaper around.

Dad says, What on **earth** has gotten into him?

Cement, → our dog

The next day, I am a little bit late for school.
        Mrs. Wilberton tells me
I have been paired up with
        Robert Granger for my project.
She's done that on purpose.
        Noah and Betty Moody
are doing a project
        on recycling,
or what to do
        with your old trash,
        i.e.,
not
        drop it
                in the
                        street.
If we drop even one piece
        my mom
        will go,
Pick that up at once,
        you litterbug.
        Sometimes
she runs after people,
        waving their trash at them.
It's very embarrassing.

Robert Granger
    is making us do a project on
Who can walk faster: a snail or a worm?
        I say,
But that's not important,
                Mrs. Wilberton.

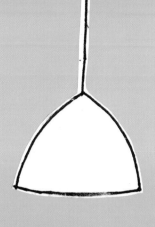

Mrs. Wilberton says,
    People who are late
for school don't have
a leg to stand on.

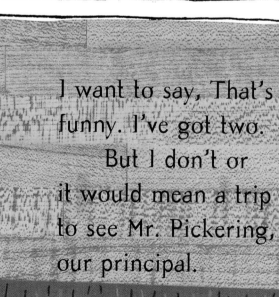

I want to say, That's
funny. I've got two.
    But I don't or
it would mean a trip
to see Mr. Pickering,
our principal.

At least things are exciting at home.

Kurt and his friend Morten are going to camp in the tree. Kurt says he's going to become an ecowarrior. He has a tent and everything.

Dad says, How are you going to **pitch** a tent in a tree?

Kurt isn't listening.

He says, **We are going to make a plan of action to stop all the destruction.**

Dad mutters, It's a **shame** he doesn't take action over all the destruction in his bedroom.

Mom says, *I'm just pleased Kurt is going to do something that involves the word action.*

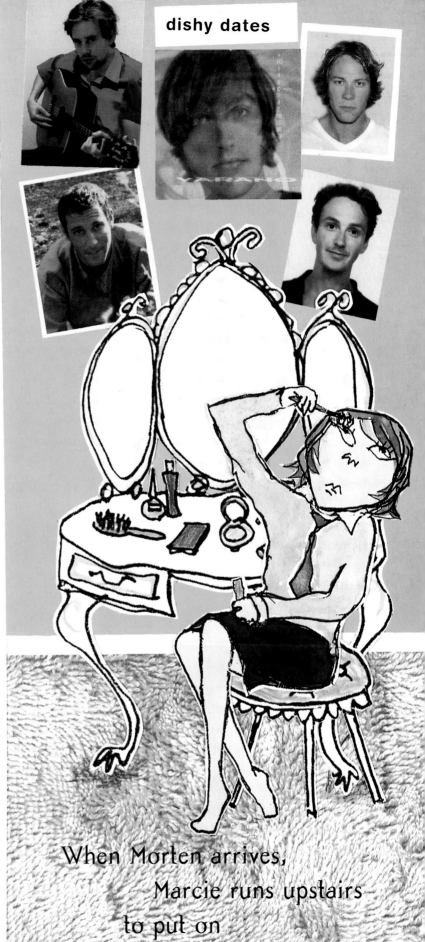

dishy dates

When Morten arrives,
Marcie runs upstairs
to put on
more makeup.

Kurt and Morten have been gone for several hours and people are beginning to worry themselves sick,

i.e., Mom.

So when it's eight o'clock we go out to see how they're doing.

They're sitting outside their tent. Grandad is there with a thermos and his friend Bert the Shirt.
We don't know why he is called Bert the Shirt. He just always is.

Then Robert Granger comes trotting along.
I just can't get rid of him.

He says,
Why is your brother camping,
Is he on vacation? **Clarice Bean?**

I say,
No one takes a vacation on their own street, nitwit.
They're having a protest.

He says,
They can't be protesting.
They don't have any signs.

Kurt gets a bit down in the mouth.
Mom tries to cheer him up. She says
she's really proud of Kurt and Morten
and pleased with what they're doing.

Marcie's just pleased
to see Morten.

So after school on Wednesday
me and Noah make some posters.
Of course Minal,
my squirty younger brother,
wants to join in.

We write, Free the Tree,
because it rhymes.

Hands Off

Noah is mostly doing the pictures.
Noah is a good drawer.
He can draw anything except
a camel or a horse.
So don't bother asking him.

Kurt is very pleased with our posters and he slightly smiles even though Minal has made a spelling mistake. And **no one** can spell the word "environment."

When we have finished, we all go down to the tree. We leave a note for Dad because, of course, he's still at the office, working like a maniac.

Free the Tree

Hands Off

When Dad gets home
he wonders where all the
quiet is coming from.
Then he sees our note.

He decides to make us
some spaghetti marinara.
(No meat because Kurt won't
eat anyone with four legs or feathers.)

Dad would much rather
cook for a living

up tree
bring
food

We are all sitting in the tree, eating spaghetti, when
suddenly someone rushes over
and takes our picture.

The next thing we know,
we are all famous in the local paper.

Hands Off

Of course
Robert Granger
gets himself in the picture.

When I get to school I am in BIG trouble.
Mrs. Wilberton wants to know why I am late **again**
and where the dickens
is my snail and worm project.

I say,
I've been up till all hours,
        saving the planet on our street.

    Mrs. Wilberton says,
        I can assure you I will be calling your mother.
    I say,
She can't get to the phone right now, Mrs. Wilberton,
                because she's up a tree.

    Mrs. Wilberton says,
    Right, that does it, young lady.
We do not tolerate nonsense in this class.

    Robert Granger says,   But it's true, **Mrs. Wilberton**.

            He shows her the picture from the paper.
            And Mrs. Wilberton looks a little
                    funny in the face.

And
that is
absolutely
the
only time
Robert
Granger
has been
useful,
ever.

My Project

This week I have been being an ecowarrior.

Free the Tree

Being an ecowarrior means you must use recycled toilet paper because toilet paper is made out of trees.